KT-385-374

FOR ELLIS, ALWAYS x

First published 2018 by Two Hoots
an imprint of Pan Macmillan
20 New Wharf Road, London N1 9RR
Associated companies throughout the world
www.panmacmillan.com
ISBN 978-1-5098-3453-2
Text and illustrations copyright © Maisie Paradise Shearring 2018
Moral rights asserted.

All rights reserved. No part of this publication may be reproduced, stored in a retrieval system, or transmitted, in any form or by any means (electronic, mechanical, photocopying, recording or otherwise), without the prior written permission of the publisher.

1 3 5 7 9 8 6 4 2
A CIP catalogue record for this book is available from the British Library.
Printed in China
The illustrations in this book were created using
paint, pencil crayons, ink, brush pens and collage.

With thanks to Suzanne Carnell, Helen Weir and Sharon King-Chai

www.twohootsbooks.com

MAISIE PARADISE SHEARRING

ANNA and OTIS

TWO HOOTS

Anna and Otis were the best of friends.
They loved exploring and spent long days
having adventures in the garden.

They had lots of fun together!

Like all best friends they
argued sometimes . . .

. . . but they always made
up very quickly.

One lazy afternoon, Anna said, "I think we
should go and explore town tomorrow, Otis.
There must be lots of new adventures to have there."

Otis didn't know what to say. He knew that some people
were scared of snakes, even harmless ones like him, so he
had never ventured further than his home or the garden.

Otis saw how Gordon from next door peered over the fence at him . . .

. . . and how the postman delivered his letters.

If this was how two people felt about him,
then what would a whole town think?

"Don't worry, Otis," said Anna. "You are brilliant.
Only silly, mean people wouldn't like
someone as great as you."

But it turned out the whole town was very silly.
And really quite mean.

Anna had never seen Otis so sad and it made
her very cross. How could people be so unkind?

"Try not to worry, Otis. People are only scared because
they've never met a snake. They just don't know you yet.
Let's be brave and try again."

Otis didn't feel very brave but he didn't want to let Anna down.

And so Anna marched straight into
the first shop she came to, which
happened to be Silvio's hairdresser's.

"Hello," Anna said, "I'd like a haircut, please,
and for my friend, Otis, one shampoo!"

Otis was very scared, but just as Anna
had told him, he smiled and said, "Hello."

Silvio cut the same people's hair all year round, and although Otis had no hair, it was actually very nice to chat to someone new.

He also looked marvellous after a shampoo!

Silvio told all his customers and friends, and they told their friends too.

Next, Anna and Otis went into Sally's Wheels.
"Hello," Anna said, "I'd like a skateboard for
me and some wheels for Otis, please!"

Once again Otis was scared, but just as
Anna had told him, he smiled and said,

Finding the perfect wheels for Otis
was a little bit trickier than usual.

But once Sally found the right ones . . .

Sally told all her friends.
And everyone at the skatepark told their friends.

Are you hungry?

Come to the park!

Look

I want to be like Otis!

Do you think I'll be able to do tricks too?

Woof!

After playing at the park, everyone invited
Anna and Otis to Lara's Café for lunch.

Making friends and being brave had made
them both very hungry!

Chef Lara was worried because she had never
made lunch for a snake before . . . but it turned
out Otis was not at all fussy about what he ate.

That night Anna invited Otis for a sleepover.
They talked and talked about their day.
It had been their biggest adventure yet!
Then at last they went to sleep,
feeling very happy.

Night, night, Anna

Sleep tight, Otis

After that, Anna and Otis continued to spend their
days together, exploring and having adventures.
Sometimes it was just the two of them.

29,
30,
31

And sometimes they went to
meet their friends in town . . .

who always made them very welcome!